Dear Parent:

You and your child are about to embark on an extraordinary adventure in learning!

Hi, I'm Woodchuck. Welcome to Peanut Butter Pond! Join my lovable, laughable friends at our forest home and we'll help develop your child's imagination and thinking skills.

Like all of the delightful Peanut Butter Pond products, my story, The Day Woodchuck Would Chuck Wood, is much more than entertainment. The storybook, audiotape, and additional activities form a true learning experience that lets your child practice the reasoning and problem-solving skills so crucial for early school success.

While I was getting ready for my winter nap, the Thinking Well people carefully sprinkled thinking questions throughout my story and audiotape. Discover how these simple, yet mind-stretching questions enrich the story, stimulate discussion, and inspire your child to ask even more questions. And my story especially helps your child to evaluate, to analyze, and to be a good problem solver!

Now, sit back with your child and enjoy! It's time to wonder and wander through Peanut Butter Pond!

Thoughtfully yours,

Woodchuck

A division of LinguiSystems, Inc.

Thinking Well
3100 4th Avenue
East Moline, IL 61244

1-800-U-2-THINK

The Day Woodchuck Would Chuck Wood

at Peanut Butter Pond

Story by Lael Littke
Illustrated by Stephanie McFetridge Britt

Everyone at Peanut Butter Pond was getting ready for winter. Up in Tall Tree, Bird happily packed his suitcase to take on his long flight south. Beaver busily checked over his dam that kept the water in the pond.

What could Beaver be looking for when he checks his dam?

Far beneath the ground, Woodchuck carefully made a bed from the dry grass he'd brought down to his den. As he worked, he sang this song:

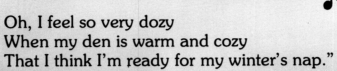

"Oh, my tummy feels so tubby
And I am so round and chubby
That I really couldn't eat another scrap.

Oh, I feel so very dozy
When my den is warm and cozy
That I think I'm ready for my winter's nap."

When Woodchuck's bed was ready, he lay down and curled himself into a fat, round ball. He yawned and closed his eyes.

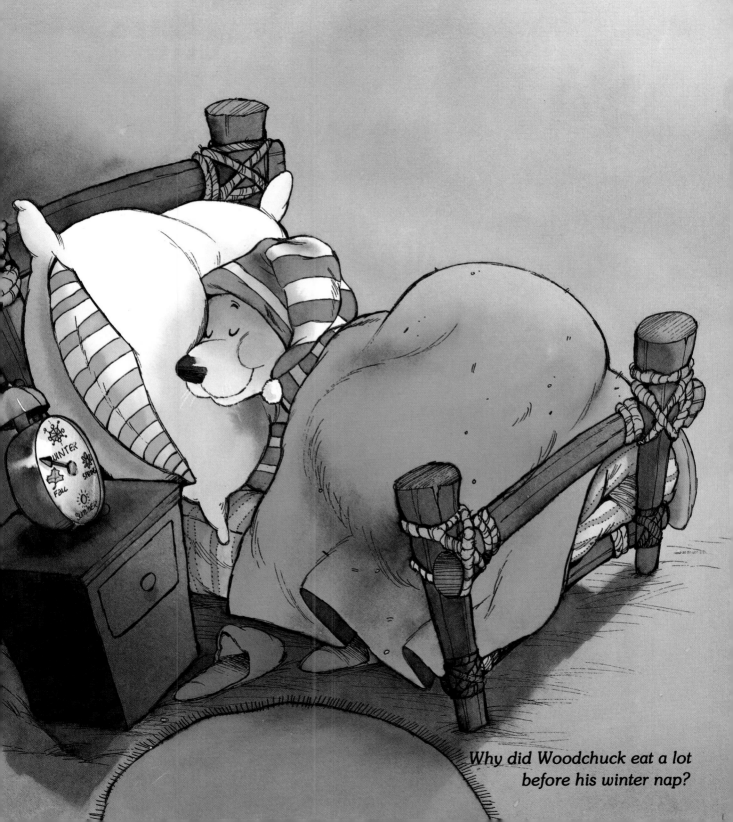

Why did Woodchuck eat a lot before his winter nap?

Just as Woodchuck started to snore, Snake came slithering swiftly down the long tunnel to his den.

"Wake up, ssssleepyhead," Snake said. "We need you up at the pond!"

"Wait until spring," Woodchuck grumbled. "I'll come up then."

Snake poked Woodchuck with his nose. "We need you now, Woodchuck. Ssssomething terrible has happened! Sssso hurry!"

Skunk was rolling one of the chunks toward the broken dam.

"Woodchuck, help me," Skunk called. "I can't do this all myself! Now is the time to find out how much wood would a woodchuck chuck if a woodchuck could chuck wood!"

Let's say it together. "How much wood would a woodchuck chuck if a woodchuck could chuck wood?" What does that mean?

Woodchuck shook his head. "I can't help you."

Skunk stopped to puff. "You could if you would, Woodchuck."

"I ssssuspect you should if you could, Woodchuck," Snake said.

"I could if I would, but I won't." Woodchuck rubbed his round tummy.
"If I chucked all that wood, I'd work off the fat I put on during the summer.
Then I wouldn't have enough fat to live on during my long winter sleep."

Bird looked worried as he flew over the broken dam.
Then he told Woodchuck,
        "If you don't respond,
          there won't be a pond."

Should Woodchuck help fix the dam? Why or why not?

Woodchuck felt cranky again. His tummy was beginning to feel rumbly, but everything he liked to eat was frozen.

"I'm going back to my den before I get so hungry I can't sleep," he muttered.

"I'll give you my food," Skunk said. "I've got some dried grubs and a juicy slug and a couple of crispy beetles!"

Woodchuck shuddered. "I'd rather starve!" He started toward his tunnel.

Why didn't Woodchuck want to eat Skunk's food?

"Wait!" yelled Bird.
        "If you go to work and chuck the wood,
        I'll bring you something very good."

"What?" Woodchuck asked suspiciously. "I don't like worms."

Bird flew down to perch on Woodchuck's shoulder.
"How about peanuts and popcorn and pizza and more!
I'll bring them all back from the General Store!"

Woodchuck's tummy growled!

Why is Woodchuck's tummy growling?

"Okay, show me where to chuck the wood," Woodchuck sighed.

Beaver stopped gnawing the logs long enough to say, "Just toss it from here to there."

From here to there was a good long way! With another sigh, Woodchuck began chucking wood.

"Whew," he said after a while. "I've already worked off a lot of my fat. I'll have to stop."

"You do sssseem sssslimmer," Snake admitted.

Why does Woodchuck think he should stop working?

From his perch on Woodchuck's shoulder, Bird whispered,
"Marshmallow goo
and chocolate, too!"

Woodchuck's tummy ROARED!

Woodchuck chucked more chunks of wood. He chucked so many that he worked off every bit of his fat. Now he was as thin as Snake.

"I can't chuck anymore," he said.

If Woodchuck is as thin as Snake, is he still a woodchuck? How do you know?

From his perch on Woodchuck's shoulder, Bird whispered,
"Ice cream so yummy
and drops that are gummy!
Masses and masses
of sticky molasses!
Hard candy mix
and cinnamon sticks!"

After twittering a few more tempting rhymes, Bird ruffled his feathers and flew away.

Woodchuck's tummy positively THUNDERED!

a gallon of fudge ripple ice cream, a pound of malted milk balls, and two dozen cinnamon sticks!

Woodchuck ate everything that was in the bag. Then, he ate the bag, too! He sighed with contentment.

Do you think Woodchuck is fat enough now to sleep all winter? Why do you think so?

"Now my tummy is tubby again. And we found out the answer to your question, Skunk."

Skunk looked puzzled. "But I didn't keep track of how much wood you chucked, Woodchuck. How much wood *could* a woodchuck chuck if a woodchuck would chuck wood?"

"ENOUGH!" Woodchuck said as he waddled toward his tunnel to start his winter's nap again. And as he waddled, Woodchuck could hear Bird twitter, "How much wood did Woodchuck chuck from here to there and more? He chucked a bunch of wood and then, he ate the General Store!"

Think 'n' Tell

Why was it so important to fix the dam at Peanut Butter Pond?

Should Woodchuck's friends have asked him to help mend the dam? Why or why not?

Suppose Woodchuck didn't help fix the dam. How would the story be different?

Pretend you are Woodchuck. What do you see in your underground home? What do you feel? What do you smell?

Pretend Woodchuck is finally sleeping, and the dam breaks again! What would happen?

Show, Don't Tell!

Snake told Woodchuck to wake up and come see ssssomething terrible. Snake didn't tell Woodchuck what the ssssomething terrible was. He showed him. Play this game and show, don't tell, your answers!

What you need: Play-Doh

What to do: Let's play a game. Listen to my questions about the story, and then, instead of telling me the answer, use Play-Doh to make the answer. Remember, you can't talk. Just use your Play-Doh to answer my questions.

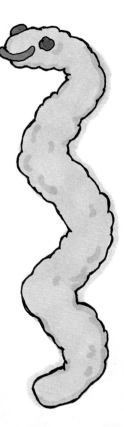

- ✿ What was Beaver fixing?
- ✿ What does Snake look like?
- ✿ Make something Woodchuck ate.
- ✿ Make your favorite Peanut Butter Pond animal.

Think of a question about the story. Ask a friend your question. Let your friend use Play-Doh to answer!

Would you rather tell or show your answer to someone? Why?

Goody Bag!

Bird brought a bag of wonderful goodies to his friend, Woodchuck. Make a special bag of your own and fill it with goodies for your friend.

What you need: lunchbag
crayons
fruits, candy, etc.

What to do:

1. Decide which friend you will give the goody bag to.

2. Use crayons to decorate the goody bag with pictures that remind you of your friend.

3. Fill the bag with goodies.

Pick a special time to give your friend the goody bag.
Say, "Thank you for being such a good friend."

What makes someone a good friend?

Woodchuck's Quilt

Woodchuck has a beautiful leaf quilt on his bed. He found those leaves on the ground at Peanut Butter Pond. You can make a beautiful leaf quilt from leaves you find in your own neighborhood.

What you need: iron   leaves   wax paper

What to do:

1. Collect leaves of different sizes, colors, and shapes.

2. Put an old towel on a flat surface. Lay a sheet of wax paper on top of the towel.

3. Overlap the leaves as you design your own leaf quilt on the wax paper.

4. Put a second sheet of wax paper over your leaf design.

5. Have your parent help you slide a hot iron across the wax paper. As the wax melts, the two sheets will melt together, holding your beautiful leaves inside!

Before your favorite stuffed animal goes to sleep tonight, cover him with your beautiful leaf quilt.

Why is it usually colder at night than during the day?

Woodchuck, Would You Chuck?